The Gatsby Kids

and the

QUEEN OF THE NILE

Book 2 in The Adventures of the
Gatsby Kids

Brian G. Michaud

This is a work of fiction. All of the characters, organizations, and
events portrayed in this novel are products of the author's
imagination.

Cover art by Clare Letendre.

THE GATSBY KIDS MEET THE QUEEN OF THE NILE

Copyright © 2018 by Brian G. Michaud

For those who want to know the unknown

Other titles by Brian G. Michaud

The Adventures of the Gatsby Kids

The Gatsby Kids and the Outlaw of Sherwood

The Gatsby Kids Meet the Queen of the Nile

The Gatsby Kids Take a Ride on the Not-So-Underground Railroad

The Gatsby Kids and the Da Vinci Trove

The Gatsby Kids Meet the King of Rock and Roll

The Tales of Gaspar

The Road to Nyn

The Ring of Carnac

A Winter's Masquerade

The Charmed Lands

Acknowledgements

This book would not be possible without the help and encouragement of those who read early editions of the manuscript. Thank you to my teacher and student friends to who took the time to comment and critique the early draft of this book. Your input help make the story come alive.

The Gatsby Kids

and the

QUEEN OF THE NILE

CHAPTER 1
A MYSTERY

You would think that spending time in a medieval dungeon would slake the appetite of any adventurer.

You would think...

As intelligent as my brothers and I supposedly are, we can't seem to stay away from getting ourselves into trouble. And that trouble usually involves traveling through time.

~ Constance Gatsby

I stood with my ear pressed to the door of my father's study. I don't usually make a habit of eavesdropping on my father's conversations, but there was something going on in that room that my brothers and I were determined to hear. We must have looked like a bizarre totem pole with me, the oldest and in eighth grade at the top, followed by seventh grade Ernest, and sixth grade George at the bottom.

"If Dad catches us snooping on him, we'll be grounded for a month," George whispered.

"Shhh. Just listen," I said.

Our father, Dr. Greyson Gatsby, is an archaeologist. Most kids wouldn't give one lick about old bones or ancient artifacts, but we're different from most kids. My brothers and I prefer reading books to playing outside, board games over video games, and dress pants rather than jeans. Yes, we are nerds. *So* nerdy that many of the other students at Belmont Junior High call us "the Geeksbys."

"I've never seen anything like it," Dad complained from the other side of the door. "It doesn't make any sense."

"Maybe it's just a design that means nothing," the voice of Mr. Fitzwaller suggested. He's the curator at The Dayton Art Institute, a museum in our home town of Dayton, Ohio. Mr. Fitzwaller is in charge of all the artwork in the museum—no piece of art enters or exits the museum without his approval.

"It's got to mean *something*," Dad insisted. "This gold pendant is from Cleopatra's private collection."

Mr. Fitzwaller took a deep breath and sighed. "Ah, Cleopatra—the Queen of the Nile—ruler of Egypt over two thousand years ago. Such a woman of intelligence and intrigue." He cleared his throat. "But that doesn't mean that the hieroglyph on that pendant has to mean something. You're always looking for a mystery, Greyson."

"What's a hieroglyph?" George whispered.

"Hieroglyphics is writing from ancient Egypt," I explained. "Each symbol, or hieroglyph, represents something, like a house or a cat."

"Yeah. Don't you know anything?" Ernest said, giving George a nudge with his elbow.

"Ow!" George grunted. He gave Ernest an elbow in return.

"Shhh. They'll hear us," I hissed. The last thing I wanted was to get caught spying on our father. He's very kind to us, but he's also a master at the "I'm disappointed in you" look. My stomach began to do flip flops with guilt just thinking about it.

"Let's keep listening," Ernest urged.

5

"It could be a hieroglyph that wasn't used very often. I'm sure you'll figure it out," Mr. Fitzwaller assured. "But I must be going now. We have a shipment of ancient Greek pottery arriving at the museum this afternoon."

We scrambled away from the door and pretended that we were walking down the hallway when Mr. Fitzwaller exited our father's study. From a distance, Mr. Fitzwaller could have been mistaken for a well-dressed kid, for he was very short and thin. But when he got closer, you couldn't help but notice the lines on his face and the pencil-thin mustache that gave him away as a fifty-something.

"Oh! Hello, children," he greeted warmly. "I didn't see you when I came in."

"We were...um...playing Scrabble in Constance's room," Ernest said.

It was somewhat true. We *had* been playing Scrabble in my room when Mr. Fitzwaller's car rolled into the driveway. But, when we heard our father greet him and then quickly and mysteriously usher him into his private study, we immediately stopped our game and snuck down the hall.

"Oh, Scrabble is one of my favorites," Mr. Fitzwaller exclaimed with a smile and a clap of his hands. "Don't forget the word 'qanat' when you're stuck with a Q and no U." With that last piece of advice, Mr. Fitzwaller showed himself to the door.

"Come on," George said, pulling Ernest and me by our shirtsleeves. "We have plans to make." He led the way back to my room and closed the door.

"What plans?" I asked.

"We're going to travel back to ancient Egypt to help Dad solve the mystery of the pendant," George said as simply as if he had just suggested going for a ride on our bikes.

Chapter 2
Making Plans

I paced back and forth in my room. "We don't even know if we can do it again," I said, shaking my head.

The "it" that I was referring to was time-travel. Two weeks earlier, the clan of bullies at our school targeted my brothers and I for the Ritual— a ridiculous tradition at Belmont Junior High in which the biggest nerds in the school (yes, that would be me and my brothers) are thrown into one of the showers in the girls' locker room and drenched with water. Strange as it may seem, that shower—along with an old English coin—sent us on an adventure that involved Robin Hood,

George being locked in a dungeon, and the creative use of bubble gum. That adventure was a secret though—a secret that we did not dare share with anyone—unless we wanted all our friends to think that we were totally out of our minds bonkers.

"We might go in the shower, turn it on, and then just come out looking like wet fools," Ernest said with his arms folded across his chest.

"If the English coin from the Middle Ages led us to Robin Hood, that pendant could take us to ancient Egypt during the time of Cleopatra," George suggested.

"Or we could wind up dead," Ernest retorted. "I've got to stay alive long enough to present my newest invention in science class. It's a self-driving lawn mower, complete with animal detection software."

"For avoiding or aiming," George asked with a mischievous grin.

I huffed. "George, sometimes I wonder about you." My little brother has the most warped sense of humor ever. I turned to Ernest, "Let's not lose focus. I think we *should* try to go back in time to ancient Egypt. What's the worst thing that could happen?"

"I've already said it," Ernest replied, throwing his arms in the air. "We could wind up dead!"

George put an arm around Ernest's shoulder. "We'll be careful. Anyway, it will be so cool! Kind of like going to Luke Skywalker's home planet of Tatooine."

Ernest and I shared a glance and rolled our eyes. George always found a way to relate everything to *Star Wars*. I wanted to jump in on the conversation, but I decided to let my brothers verbally duke it out for a bit longer.

"Even if we *can* travel over two thousand years back in time to ancient Egypt, how are we going to figure out what the hieroglyph on that pendant means?" Ernest asked.

"Maybe we can ask somebody?" George suggested.

"Oh, yeah," Ernest scoffed. "We'll just go up to Cleopatra and say, 'Hey, Cleo. Don't ask us how we got a hold of your jewelry, but could you explain this to us?'"

"Will we be able to speak their language?" I wondered aloud. "The coin that we brought back to medieval England allowed us to communicate with Robin Hood and Little John, but remember what happened when we got separated? We had a hard time understanding what Robin Hood was saying. It's a good thing that Middle English isn't too far removed from Modern English, but none of us speak Greek."

"Greek? I thought we were going to Egypt where they speak—you know—Egyptian." George said.

"The common people did," I replied.

"Then why are we talking about Greek?" George asked.

"The pharaohs of that time spoke Greek. Cleopatra's family was descended from Alexander the Great's general, Ptolemy of Lagus, who was Greek…well, Macedonian to be specific. The Ptolemies ruled from the Egyptian city of Alexandria, which was named after Alexander the Great and located in the Nile River delta."

George shook his head. "This is confusing."

"We'll just have to make sure that we don't get separated so that we understand what people are saying to us," I said.

"Wait a minute!" Ernest interrupted. "You're talking as if we're actually going to do this. And I've already told you—I'm not going!"

"It would help Dad," I urged. I knew it was crazy, but I actually agreed with George on this one. I wanted to go.

"We could wind up dead!" Ernest said (for the third time, if I haven't lost count). "The ancient Egyptians were not exactly friendly to foreign visitors." He walked over to my bookshelf and took down a book entitled *The History of Ancient Egypt*. "Let's see…slavery…cutting off your ears if you're caught stealing… Ah! Here's a picture showing Cleopatra testing poison on prisoners.

That sounds pleasant, doesn't it? Oh, wait. It gets better. It says here that she married her brothers."

"Brothers? As in plural? Yuck!" George exclaimed. "That's just wrong!"

Ernest slammed the book down on the table. "I'm not going," he stated firmly.

"Fine. Stay here by yourself," George said. "I'm ready for an adventure. Luke Skywalker wouldn't turn down the chance to go to ancient Egypt."

"That's only because he was from a desert planet," Ernest retorted.

"You guys are talking like *Star Wars* is real," I snorted.

"Bite your tongue," George interrupted. "Don't go slamming my *Star Wars* buddies."

I sighed. "Can we stay on topic? Are we going to do this or not?"

George got up and began pacing back and forth. "I only see one problem."

"Only one?" Ernest asked, arching an eyebrow.

George ignored Ernest's comment and said, "Look at us."

We looked at each other. We all wore khaki pants, blue button-down shirts, and plaid tweed jackets—a custom that often got us shoved into lockers by the bullies at school.

"We don't exactly look like ancient Egyptians," I admitted.

Our unusual style of dressing was a quirk that we did for as long as we could remember and was mostly due to the insistence of our nanny, Miss Hobbes.

Our mother, Emily, passed away shortly after George was born. Miss Hobbes helped take care of us since we were all still in diapers. She had also been our mother's nanny, so Miss Hobbes is like our cranky, but loving, grandmother. She claims that worrying about clothes and hairstyles is for the weak-minded and that always dressing the same saves time and energy. "Time is your most precious commodity," she always says. Whatever that means…

I opened *The History of Ancient Egypt* and began leafing through its pages. It didn't take me long to find what I was looking for. "I bet we could make outfits like these." I slid the book across the table and pointed to a picture of a man and a woman. "The woman's dress is called a *kalasiris*, and the man is wearing a long tunic."

"I'm not wearing that!" Ernest exclaimed. "We'll look like Miss Hobbes when she goes to the beach."

"So does that mean you're coming with us?" George asked with a smirk.

Chapter 3
A Strange Way to Take a Shower

So, under duress and against my better judgement, I decided to go with my misguided siblings.

~ Ernest Gatsby

You would have no fun if it weren't for us. You should be saying "Thank you."

~ George Gatsby

I should be looking in the classifieds for a new brother and sister.

~ Ernest Gatsby

Can I please continue the story?

~ Constance Gatsby

One week later, my brothers and I arrived at school early and crept through the eerily quiet halls of Belmont Jr. High.

For some strange reason, I had been thinking about my mother all morning. Maybe it was a dream that I had—you know, the kind that leaves an impression, but you can't quite grasp what it was about. A wave of sadness passed over me. I missed my mother. Even though I didn't really remember her, I missed her.

I felt like I knew her from the pictures I had of her. She was always smiling. She must have loved life. Her smiles were real—like she was laughing—not those fake "stare at the camera smiles" that I give each year on school picture day.

"It's weird when nobody's around," George said, breaking in on my thoughts.

I nodded and walked a little quicker toward the gym. We entered with our duffle bags slung over our shoulders.

I felt bad that we had lied to Miss Hobbes. We told her that we had to get to school before everybody else to prepare for a presentation on ancient Egypt. Strangely, Miss Hobbes hadn't seemed surprised and had even offered to help us, giving suggestions on our sandal designs.

Pushing open the door to the girls' locker room, we stopped and listened.

Silence.

"Good. Nobody's here," I whispered.

Our destination was at the end of row upon row of old grey lockers—a shower with a plastic curtain covered in yellow smiley faces. We snuck in and put our bags down on one of the benches. I opened mine to make sure that Cleopatra's pendant was still there. Our father had left early for a meeting at the museum and wouldn't be back until suppertime. We had plenty of time to "borrow" the ancient artifact from his study and return it before he came home.

We pulled our Egyptian clothes from our bags and put them on. I tucked the pendant in a secret pocket that I had sewed on the inside of my robe.

"You two look ridiculous," George said, laughing and pointing at Ernest and I.

"And you look like you got into a fight with your bed sheets—and *lost*," Ernest replied.

"I think you have it on backwards," I said, adjusting George's clothing.

We gathered in the shower stall behind the multitude of smiley faces.

Ernest sighed. "Well, here we go again."

"Can we at least try it with warm water this time?" George pleaded.

I nodded and twisted the lever to the halfway position.

The water sprayed all over us. We waited, but, other than getting our costumes soaking wet, nothing happened.

"It's not working," George said.

"No kidding," Ernest huffed, giving George a shove.

"Knock it off, you two," I snapped. "That isn't helping."

I didn't want to admit it to my brothers, but I was starting to feel uneasy. Could we have just imagined our adventure with Robin Hood? Had somebody played an elaborate trick on us? Were we crazy for thinking that we could travel through time to anywhere that we wished to go?

"Do you think we have to be wearing our regular clothes?" George asked.

"It's worth a try," I said with a shrug, trying not to sound nervous, anxious, and depressed all at once. "But let's just put them over these robes if we can. We don't know who will be around or how fast we'll have to change when we get to Egypt."

"*If* we get to Egypt," Ernest mumbled.

My brothers and I stepped out of the shower dripping wet and put on our shirts, shoes, and jackets over our Egyptian robes. I felt totally disgusting—like a giant, tightly-wrapped, soggy sausage.

George laughed. "You look like a pair of overstuffed scarecrows."

"Have *you* looked in a mirror," Ernest asked.

"Come on. Let's try it again," I said, stepping in between my brothers.

We reentered the shower stall, and I turned the handle once again. A stream of water engulfed us. The flow increased to a deluge. The water rose up to our ankles, then our knees, then our waists. Suddenly, the floor dropped from below us, and the warm water rushed over our heads like a flood!

Chapter 4
Not So Welcome in Egypt

I fought against the weight of my wet clothing and swam with all my might. My head broke the surface of the water, and I took thankful gulps of air. Looking around, I saw my brothers bobbing on either side of me. We were floating near the shore of a narrow canal. Palm trees and tall reeds lined its banks. Beyond the trees were rows of mud-brick houses.

"What are you doing in the canal?" a woman's voice called out. A bronze-skinned, middle-aged woman stood on the bank and waved a large sheet of white linen.

I almost jumped out of my skin at the sound of her voice. *Did she see us appear out of nowhere? Who was she? Would she start screaming for help?* If the river turned to ice, it wouldn't have frozen my blood so fast.

"She must be washing her clothes," Ernest said, nodding toward the basket on the ground next to the woman. The basket was overflowing with soiled white linens.

I took another look at the woman. She seemed more annoyed than anything else. Kind of like Miss Hobbes when she's told us for the thousandth time how to fold the laundry the correct way.

I was beginning to feel relieved until she said, "Don't you know there are crocodiles nearby?"

Relief turned to fright. My brothers and I kicked and screamed all the way to shore.

"Thanks for the warning," I panted as I leaned on a wooden cart filled with baskets of linen.

"We kind of got a little lost," Ernest said.

"Yeah, we're not from around here," George admitted.

The woman didn't say anything, but looked each of us up and down. Suddenly she broke her silence. "You are not Egyptian, although you speak our language perfectly."

"Sure, we're Egyptian," George asserted.

"Really? I've never seen clothing like yours," the woman said.

We looked at our plaid tweed jackets. Then we looked at the woman's simple white robe. Swiftly and wordlessly, we took off our outer clothes and stuffed them into our duffel bags.

"There. Is that better?" George asked.

The woman held her bronze-skinned arm alongside George's arm. "A little. But I've never met an Egyptian with skin so white."

"Um…they make really good sunblock in our village," George said hesitantly.

Ernest and I looked at each other with concern. If this simple washerwoman saw through our disguise, we would have no chance of fooling one of Egypt's most intelligent queens.

"You three boys—" the woman began.

"I'm a girl!" I insisted, cutting the woman off. I wore my hair very short and was often mistaken for a boy—to my great annoyance. *This year, I should finally let my hair grow out.* I made a mental note to ask Miss Hobbes to cancel my next haircut appointment.

"Oh, so you are," the woman said, squinting at me. "As I was saying, you three *children* better be careful. The only ones I have ever seen with skin like yours have come over in the galley boats—as slaves."

"Uh, we're not—" I began, but it was the Egyptian's turn to cut me off.

"You'd better hand me those strange sacks of yours," the washerwoman said, looking over her shoulder and down the road. "Here comes His Highness, the Prince!"

It probably wasn't the smartest thing to trust a total stranger with our only ticket home, but we didn't exactly have time to discuss our options. I handed the washerwoman my duffel bag, and my brothers did the same. The woman deftly stuffed them underneath her pile of soiled clothing not a moment too soon.

A short distance away, a large group of people surrounded a litter that was being carried by twelve men down a wide avenue. (If you've never seen a litter, imagine taking a big fancy chair and covering it with a large square umbrella. Then attach poles to it so your friends can carry you. That is, *if* your friends will carry you.) Women waved gigantic palm fronds to cool the rider of the chair, and a harpist walked alongside singing a strangely beautiful song—it sounded weird to my ears, but it was probably one of ancient Egypt's greatest hits.

The prince of Egypt was a boy about ten-years-old, but he had the aloof and commanding air of a king—and he was staring straight at us!

CHAPTER 5
A NOT-SO-PRINCELY PRINCE

"Quick! Pretend that you are helping me," the washerwoman instructed. She handed each of us a piece of soiled clothing and a stone. "Start scrubbing them in the canal."

My brothers and I wordlessly obeyed the woman. We bent down, dunked the linens in the water, and scrubbed vigorously.

A blend of chatter and singing echoed through the air as the pharaoh's son and his entourage approached. When the chair passed alongside us, the prince's commanding voice called for a halt.

"Hail, washerwoman!" the prince called out.

"I am at your bidding, Prince Ptolemy," the washerwoman said (pronouncing his name *TOL-eh-me*) and then bowed down to the ground.

My knees turned to jelly. What were we thinking? We didn't even have a plan. Did we actually think we were going to able to look around the city like tourists without anybody wondering who we were? Ugh! Now we had to try and fool the Prince of Egypt.

I pulled my brothers down, copying the washerwoman's prostrate position. I dared a quick peek up at the prince. He was glaring at our group with a nasty scowl on his face.

This was not good.

"Does it now take four slaves to do the work of one?" Prince Ptolemy sneered. "Each day I pass by here and see you washing your master's linens in the river, yet today you now have three other slaves helping you."

"They are new," the woman answered without looking up.

"I can see that. Their lily-white skin tells the story," the prince said. "Do you think I am stupid?"

"You are most wise, my Prince," the woman said with a tremble in her voice.

Prince Ptolemy snapped his fingers. Three men carrying spears and wearing only loincloths rushed to his side. The prince pointed at my brothers and me. "Take these slaves and bring them with us to the palace. We could use a few more servants. I had to dispose of some recently for attempting to steal from me."

"Dispose?" George whispered.

"He probably means *kill*," Ernest answered.

I gulped. No. This definitely was not good.

The prince's soldiers yanked Ernest, George, and me to our feet.

Whether we liked it or not, we were now officially Egyptian slaves.

Chapter 6

A Whole Lot of Ptolemies

The blazing Egyptian sun beat down on us as the prince's soldiers led us away from the canal.

"Anyone have a water bottle?" George panted. "How about maybe a can of Coke?"

One of the soldiers gave George a sidelong glance and shook his head with a confused grimace.

"We've got a big problem," Ernest said.

"Really? I didn't notice," George answered rolling his eyes and gesturing to the soldiers and their razor-sharp spears.

"Bigger than being captured?" I asked.

"Yes," Ernest answered.

"Bigger than being skewered?" George asked.

"Yes," Ernest replied again. "What are we going to do about our clothes? I don't think we can travel back home without them."

"Oh, I didn't think of that," George admitted.

"Of course, you didn't," Ernest snapped back. "You never think."

"Enough!" I scolded. "This isn't helping anything. Let's hope that we can find a way to get back to the canal. Prince Ptolemy said that he saw the washerwoman there every day. We'll hopefully be able to find her again."

The city's palaces and temples towered over us. The buildings were painted in vibrant shades of red, yellow, green, and blue. Seagulls flew overhead, a telling sign that the ocean was nearby.

"Wow! What's that?" George asked, pointing to a giant tower in the distance. Every once in a while, a bright light flashed from the top.

"That's one of the Seven Wonders of the Ancient World," I answered. "It's the Lighthouse of Alexandria."

"It looks more like a skyscraper," George said.

"Think of it as the world's first skyscraper. Which it kind of was. It stood over 400 feet high," I said.

"I wonder what's making the light," Ernest said. "They didn't have electricity in ancient Egypt."

"You can look it up on the Internet when we get back home," I suggested.

Ernest pursed his lips. "If we get back home."

"Hey, that thing over there looks like the Washington monument!" George exclaimed, pointing to the newest feature that caught his eye.

A tall stone column with a triangular top decorated the center of an intersection. It rested on a pedestal, and colorful hieroglyphics covered its surface.

"That's an obelisk, George," Ernest said, sounding exasperated. "And stop looking around like a tourist."

"I don't care what it *is*. I'm telling you what it *looks* like." George folded his arms and turned away from Ernest. "So, where are the pyramids?"

"There aren't any pyramids here in Alexandria. Most of the pyramids are located near Cairo and to the south. The closest one is over a hundred miles away," I explained.

"You mean we traveled all the way here, and I don't get to see a pyramid!" George exclaimed. "What a gyp!"

"Look over there," I said, pointing to a building with gigantic columns and a towering statue of a woman in front. "I think that's a temple to the goddess, Isis. Later in her life, Cleopatra took on the goddess's persona. She made the Egyptians call her the New Isis, and she dressed in special robes and jewelry to make her subjects think that she was a god."

"Talk about a superiority complex," Ernest snorted.

We rounded a corner and came within sight of the main palace of Alexandria.

"Wow!" George gasped. "It looks like the White House. Only it's got giant statues in

41

front…and it's made of stone…and it's not white…"

"So what you're saying it that it looks nothing like the White House," Ernest said dryly.

The prince's entourage traveled under a huge stone archway and into the main throne room. Servants rushed to and fro while soldiers stood rigid and watched every move that took place before them. Each soldier held a large spear with a frighteningly sharp blade.

At the end of the room, a middle-aged man and a girl about seventeen-years-old sat on stone thrones. Both wore a *pschent*,[1] the double crown of Egypt—kind of a hat within a hat—marking them as the rulers of Egypt.

"That must be the pharaoh, Ptolemy, and his daughter, Cleopatra," I whispered.

---

[1] Pronounced *skent*.

"I thought the prince's name was Ptolemy," George said.

"It is," I said. "Most of the men in this dynasty are called Ptolemy. The pharaoh is Ptolemy XII, and the prince is Ptolemy XIII. Cleopatra will eventually have a son and name him Ptolemy XV."[2]

"Wait," Ernest interrupted. "What happened to Ptolemy XIV?"

"That's her youngest brother," I answered.

"This is confusing," George complained.

"Well, at least you won't forget their names," I said with a wry grin.

"I'm just going to call the pharaoh Big Ptol, and the prince Little Ptol," George said. "If we

---

[2] Roman numerals after a monarch's name means the order in which they were born and/or ruled. Ptolemy XII means Ptolemy the 12th, Ptolemy XIII means Ptolemy the 13th, Ptolemy XIV means Ptolemy the 14th, and Ptolemy XV means Ptolemy the 15th. Cleopatra, by the way, was Cleopatra VII (7th). See the end of the book for a full explanation…and a football quiz. ☺

meet her youngest brother, I'll call him Tiny Ptol."

Ernest rolled his eyes. "You're going to get thrown in the dungeon."

Prince Ptolemy (or "Little Ptol" as George would call him) directed his servants to bring his litter directly before the throne. As we approached, I could see a scowl cross the face of the pharaoh.

"Is my son so lazy that he cannot walk in the palace?" Big Ptol asked.

"I'm not being lazy, father," Little Ptol retorted. "Why waste the work the slaves can do? We have them, so they should be working all the time." The prince waved his hand, signaling his slaves to place his litter on the ground.

The pharaoh shook his head. "This is one of the many reasons why your sister, Cleopatra, is my co-ruler and not you."

Prince Ptolemy looked as if he had been slapped in the face, but he immediately regained his composure. He smiled forcefully and then addressed the pharaoh. "Why are you so mean to me when I come bearing gifts for my honored father?"

"Gifts?" Big Ptol asked, his eyes narrowing suspiciously.

The prince motioned to my brothers and me. "I found them by the river. They were assisting a woman washing clothes in the canal, but I thought we could make better use of them here in the palace."

The pharaoh eyed us as if he was examining a used car he was thinking of buying. "With pale complexions like theirs, they must have recently come from somewhere across the Great Green Sea[3], like Gaul or Germania." He nodded and then smiled at his son. "We'll put them to work."

Cleopatra suddenly spoke up. "*If* they understand us. Slaves are only useful in the palace if they speak Greek."

"Hey, you were right about the Greek thing," George whispered to me.

"Speak only when you are spoken to!" Cleopatra commanded harshly.

We stiffened and closed our mouths tightly.

"Do you speak Greek?" Cleopatra asked.

"Um…" I hesitated. "A little…I think." I understood everything that Cleopatra was saying, so I guessed that the power of the pendant

---

[3] The Ancient Egyptians called the Mediterranean Sea the "Wodj-Wer" which translates to "The Great Green."

allowed us to speak and understand whatever language was being spoken.

"How about Egyptian?" Cleopatra asked.

"Ugh!" Little Ptol spat. "Why do you care if they speak the language of the commoners?"

"The commoners are the people we rule," Cleopatra snapped back. "If you do not care about them or their language and customs, why do you want to rule them?"

The prince appeared lost for an answer; he just huffed and folded his arms.

George took the opportunity to speak up. "We can speak Egyptian, too."

Cleopatra's eyes widened in surprise. She turned to her father. "I think my brother has brought us a truly valuable gift. These must be well-educated children to speak both Greek and Egyptian fluently."

She looked thoughtfully at my brothers and me. "I have not met anyone so educated since—"

"Yourself, smarty pants," Little Ptol interrupted.

"No," Cleopatra shot back. "I was thinking of someone else." Addressing my brothers and I, she asked, "Where are you from to be so educated?"

Ernest decided to jump into the conversation. "We're from the city of Dayton. It's very far away from here."

"Day-ton," Cleopatra said slowly as if tasting the word. "I have never heard of this city. Have you, Father?"

The pharaoh shook his head.

George nudged me.

I ignored my little brother.

George nudged me again.

"Knock it off," I said through gritted teeth, trying not to move my mouth. Ernest was right, George was going to get us thrown in the dungeon.

George nudged me a third time.

I glared at George, but he nodded his head toward Cleopatra and then scratched his neck.

I sighed with frustration and casually turned my glance toward the young pharaoh. That's when I saw it. My breath caught in my throat, and my eyes must have bulged out of my head. At the base of Cleopatra's neck was a pendant. The same pendant that I had in my pocket!

Chapter 7
And Then There Were Two

So there we were, slaves and in the possession of one of the most nefarious—that means "mean and nasty," George—rulers of all time.

Thanks for talking us into this. I owe you one.

~ Ernest Gatsby

First, I know what "nefarious" means. Second, it's not my fault. I didn't force you to go.

Pbbbt! That means "I don't care what you think."

~ George Gatsby

Can you two knock it off so I can finish the story?

~ Constance Gatsby

Let me take it from here, since this is the part of the story where you deserted us.

~ Ernest Gatsby

What?

~Constance Gatsby

The pharaoh's soldiers led us out of the throne room and into an open courtyard where dozens of children were busy scrubbing dirty bowls and plates. A cranky woman in a white robe addressed the soldiers. Her thick layer of pancake make-up made her face look like a mask.

"What do we have here?" she asked. "New slaves?"

"They're all yours, Nefreti," one of the soldiers grunted, shoving us forward. The men left, leaving my siblings and I under the woman's appraising gaze.

51

Nefreti scowled. "Scrawny little things, come with me." She marched over to a water trough. A large, precariously-stacked pile of dirty plates and bowls teetered nearby.

"Clean," she ordered and walked away.

I looked at the caked-on grime and unknown gobs of dried food, and my whole body shuddered. I hate doing dishes at home—and that's when I know whose filth I'm cleaning. This was just revolting.

As soon as Nefreti was out of earshot, George blurted out, "Dad was right! That pendant really did belong to Cleopatra!" Leave it to my brother to get excited at a time like this.

Constance nodded eagerly then added, "Maybe someone in the palace will know what the symbol means."

I groaned inwardly. *Ugh, now it's two against one.* Why can't my siblings be cynical when they need to be?

"Clean!" Nefreti yelled from the other side of the courtyard.

"If we're so valuable, why are we delegated to KP duty?" I asked. Using the tips of two fingers, I tentatively lifted an earthenware bowl and dipped it in the trough.

"Beats me," George replied. He grabbed a clay pot and dunked it heartily. Dirty water splashed on my robe and face.

"Gross! Watch what you're doing!" I seethed.

"I wouldn't complain," Constance said. "It's a good thing that they placed us together." She patted the secret pocket of her robe. "Without this pendant close by, we wouldn't understand a thing anybody says to us."

"Yeah, it seems that they hear whatever language they expect us to speak," George noted. "I didn't do anything different when they asked us to speak Egyptian." He hummed thoughtfully as he scrubbed the pot. "I wonder if there's anything in Dad's collection that would help me get through sixth grade Spanish."

"He's got some artifacts from the reign of Ferdinand and Isabella," Constance noted. "But you'd have to pass Spanish class in 1492."

George snapped his fingers. "Maybe that can be the next place we go."

I couldn't believe what I was hearing. Frustrated to no end, I dropped my bowl in the water. "You two can't be serious. After this, I'm done with time-traveling."

"More washing and less talking, slaves!" Nefreti yelled.

I jumped at the sudden shout and looked over my shoulder at the taskmaster.

Nefreti wore an even bigger scowl than before, but that wasn't what made me shudder. Beyond her, a rather large Egyptian man wearing a loincloth and holding a leather whip approached.

"You, the boy with the long hair," he said pointing at Constance. "The pharaoh wants to see you."

"I'm a girl," she said, throwing her hands on her hips.

The Egyptian shrugged. "Hmmm, that's what the pharaoh thought, too. But I doubted it."

"I've been saying for years that she needs to change her hairstyle," George whispered to me.

I stood defensively in front of Constance and craned my neck up at the big Egyptian. "Why does Pharaoh Ptolemy want to see my sister?"

"Not Pharaoh Ptolemy. Pharaoh Cleopatra," the man corrected. "She commanded me, and I don't ask questions. Neither should you." With the ease of brushing away a gnat, he pushed me aside and grabbed Constance by the arm.

Constance motioned to George and I. "Can they come with me?"

The Egyptian shook his head. "Just you."

Constance swallowed hard. Her face drooped as she looked at George and I.

"We'll be okay," George assured her. "Go ahead," he added with a shooing gesture. My brother was overconfident, as usual.

Constance nodded then followed the Egyptian out of the courtyard and into the palace.

"Now what?" George asked.

I looked around the courtyard and listened. As Constance and the pendent moved farther away, the hum of the other children's conversations gradually became unintelligible. "What do you think they'll do with us when they discover that we can't speak Egyptian or Greek?"

George dunked a plate into the trough's dirty water. "Well, since we understood them before, they'll probably think that we *do* understand them and that we're just *pretending* not to understand them."

"And that won't go over so well," I said.

"Nope."

For once, George actually looked nervous. And that made me feel even worse.

Chapter 8

Into the Lioness' Den

And so I left my brothers behind and followed the big Egyptian through the palace. I had no idea what I was getting into...and it was a good thing I didn't because I would have turned tail and ran away as fast as I could.

~ Constance Gatsby

I gawked at the gigantic painted statues that towered over us along the hallways. All the pictures that I had ever seen in books showed Egyptian statues carved of plain, colorless stone. I never imagined that the ancient Egyptians painted them in such vibrant colors. In fact, the entire palace was covered with reds, blues, and yellows. Murals adorned the walls, and colorful mosaic tiles decorated the floor.

We traveled through many corridors and up a set of wide stairs. At the top of the stairs, the man stopped.

"These are Pharaoh Cleopatra's private chambers. I must leave you here," he said. Without another word, the man turned and walked back the way we had come.

I took a tentative step down the hall. There were several rooms on each side of the corridor. Red silk curtains hung in front of archway, hiding what lay beyond.

"Hello?" I called softly. "Anybody here?"

The curtain on my left moved suddenly, and I let out a startled yelp.

A young girl in a white robe held the curtain aside.

"The pharaoh will see you in here," the girl said shyly. "Enter."

I stepped past the girl and into what appeared to be Cleopatra's bedroom. The Queen of the Nile lay sprawled on a set of pillows while nibbling on a small, reddish-orange fruit served to her by another white-robed girl.

When the young pharaoh saw me, she smiled. "Ah, you're here." She clapped her hands and directed the other two girls, "Nedjem, Aisha, leave us."

Cleopatra waved me over to her. "Would you like a fig?" she asked indicating a pile of the fruits on a silver tray.

"Um, sure." I tentatively selected a small fruit. I took a bite and did my best not to make a grimace. *Yuck!* I thought. *These taste nothing like Fig*

Newtons. Then aloud, I asked, "Your Highness, why did you want to see me?"

Cleopatra's smile immediately changed to a frown. "It is not the place for a slave to question her master," she said icily.

I dropped the fig. Bending down to pick it up with shaky hands, I thought, *I'm going to have to be careful what I say.* I stood straight and waited for the young queen to speak.

Cleopatra wore a white and blue robe; it was so clean it seemed to shine. She had exchanged her crown for a *uraeus*[4]—a golden circlet with three cobras. Bracelets dangled from each of her wrists, and the pendant hung around her neck. No matter how much I tried to force my eyes away from it, I couldn't help but let my gaze stray to the mysterious artifact that brought us here.

---

[4] Pronounced "u-REE-es"

"You like my jewelry," Cleopatra said, touching the pendant. "Maybe you will someday wear some. My family likes to give our favored servants gifts of jewelry."

I remained silent but smiled, hoping this was the proper response.

"I called you here, because you and your brothers interest me," Cleopatra continued. "Oh, don't look so startled, I can tell you are related. You look so much alike. If they're not your brothers, then they are your cousins."

"They are my brothers," I acknowledged, afraid to say any more than necessary.

"You interest me because I want to know your story. You speak Egyptian and Greek fluently. Children who know multiple languages usually come from royal households, yet you do not carry yourself as a royal."

"No, we are not royals," I answered.

The queen frowned. "Well? Are you going to make me guess?" she snapped.

I gulped. "Um, no. We are…um…from Dayton—"

"I already knew that."

"And our father…um…he's an…" I paused. I couldn't say that my father was an archaeologist. The queen would probably think that I made up the word and go into a rage. An idea came to me, and I said more confidently, "Our father deals with goods and precious items from around the world."

"Ah, so your father is a merchant," the queen smiled. "A very rich merchant, I would guess."

"We do okay." I thought of my house in Dayton, Ohio and all the modern devices. Televisions, computers, electric lights, cell

64

phones, and video games would seem like magic to the ancient Egyptians.

Cleopatra stared at me and said nothing for a while. The pharaoh just nibbled on her figs. I was afraid to say anything, so I stood silently until she spoke again.

"I also summoned you here because one of my servants overheard your conversation with your brothers."

The blood froze in my veins. Which conversation could Cleopatra be referring to? Did she think that we came here to steal her pendant? Did we let anything slip about traveling through time?

"You have the gift of prophecy," Cleopatra said gently.

"The gift of *what?*" I asked, almost choking on the last bit of fig that I had been nibbling.

Cleopatra slammed her hands on her pillows. "Don't toy with me, slave!"

I took an involuntary step backward. *Wow! Somebody's got anger management issues.*

The young pharaoh went on. "You made a prophecy—a prediction—about me when you were in the throne room."

I thought back on our audience with Cleopatra and her father. *What did I predict? Let's see. We entered the throne room. Ernest and George were asking me about the pharaohs' names and... Uh, oh...*

"You prophesized that I would someday have a son and name him Ptolemy. Did you not?" The Egyptian queen's gaze seemed to pierce my very soul.

I hesitated. "W-would you believe a lucky guess? I mean, all the boys in your family are named Ptolemy."

"Yes, but how do you know I will have a son and not a daughter?"

"Well, I…um…"

"What else do you know about me?" Cleopatra leaned forward on her cushions. "You are not just a merchant's daughter. You are a prophet." Her eyes narrowed like that of a cobra about to strike. "So…make a prophecy."

"I…uh…" I couldn't figure out what to say or do. I didn't think it was a good idea to tell Cleopatra something about her future. She might try to make it happen too soon and alter history. Or she could avoid doing it and change history another way.

The young pharaoh reached under one of her cushions and pulled out a jeweled flask. "Let me make this a little clearer for you. If you don't start prophesying right now, I'm going to use this poison on your brothers. I'll start with the younger one."

CHAPTER 9
A MYSTERIOUS DISCOVERY

"I-I…" I stammered.

"Sister, I need to speak with you," someone said from the doorway.

I whirled at the unexpected voice.

Prince Ptolemy stood in the doorway with an impatient expression on his face.

I never thought I would be happy to see Little Ptol, but the interruption was just what I needed. It gave me the opportunity to think of what I could tell Cleopatra.

"I will right back," Cleopatra said. "Wait right here." She accentuated the last word by extending her finger like an arrow at my feet.

Cleopatra exited with her brother, leaving me alone in her bedroom. Not daring to move, I stood rooted in place and searched my memory for facts about Cleopatra.

1. Cleopatra will eventually marry both of her brothers.

Yuck! That won't do.

2. Cleopatra will test out poisons on her slaves.

Hmmm, she probably already does that, so it wouldn't be a prediction.

3. In the not-to-distant future, Cleopatra's father will die, her brother will take over the kingdom, and she will go into exile for a number of years.

Nope. I don't think she reacts well to bad news.

4. Julius Caesar will someday be her boyfriend.

Now that one has potential.

In my nervousness, I began to pace back and forth. It's what I do when I need to think. My hand strayed into the pocket of my *kalasiris*. I felt the cold metal of the pendant, and I wondered anew what secret the queen's jewelry held. Cleopatra obviously liked it or she wouldn't be wearing it. I doubted that the queen did anything that she didn't want to do.

I stepped out onto the wide balcony. A breathtaking view of the city and its busy harbor stretched out below me. The gigantic Lighthouse of Alexandria stood like a sentinel presiding over the Egyptians' comings and goings. I let the breeze blow through my hair and tried not to think that my brothers' lives were on the line.

Sighing, I stepped back into the room. Paintings and hieroglyphics covered the walls of Cleopatra's bedroom. The pictures seemed to depict the story of Cleopatra's life. One of the scenes showed Cleopatra as a baby with her parents standing over her like giants and many tiny people celebrating her birth.[5] I half-heartedly scanned the images on the wall. Cleopatra wearing a crown. Cleopatra sailing on a galley boat. Cleopatra walking through the fields while farmers tended to the crops.

Ugh! What an egomaniac! Who covers their walls with pictures of themselves?

Suddenly, one small picture made my heart skip a beat. There, in an inconspicuous corner, was the image of Cleopatra standing next to a very tiny person. Although Cleopatra was painted with beautiful colors, my attention was drawn to the smaller figure and the curious way the little woman was dressed. However, it wasn't only the

---

[5] Ancient Egyptian art showed important people, such as pharaohs, as very big and common people as very small.

figures that excited me—it was the image above them.

"It's almost like the pendant, but it's upside down," I said in awe. I took the piece of jewelry out of my pocket.

My heart beat wildly. "We've been looking at it the wrong way!" I examined the loop at the top where the chain was meant to pass through. "But that doesn't make sense. The pendant obviously hung this way."

"What are you doing, slave!"

Cleopatra stood in the doorway. And she didn't look happy.

Chapter 10
The Prediction

I yelped and quickly stuffed the pendant back in my pocket, but the young pharaoh was not looking my way. Cleopatra was glaring at someone else down the hallway.

Two men stepped into the room carrying a large bundle between them.

"I'm sorry, My Queen," one of the men said, "but this rug is much heavier than it looks. We are delivering it to your chamber as you commanded."

"Put it down and leave us," Cleopatra barked.

The men placed the rug in the center of the room and departed hastily.

Cleopatra stepped over the rug and approached me. The young pharaoh looked directly into my eyes as if she were going to hypnotize me. "Now, my little seer, you will make a prophecy for me. Tell me more of my future."

"I need time and space to concentrate," I said.

I knew that I had to make this look like the real deal. Fortune tellers usually looked into a crystal ball or traced the lines in a person's palm. I didn't have a crystal ball, and I was afraid that there might be a punishment for touching the pharaoh. Looking at the cushions, I decided that would be a good place to meditate. I attempted to sit down, but Cleopatra screamed.

"Do you dare sit on the bedding of a queen?"

"U-um, no. Of course not," I stammered. "The power of prophecy is making my vision hazy. How about if I just sit on this rolled up rug?"

"That will be fine," Cleopatra said. She waved her hand, indicating that I was allowed to sit.

I flopped down on the rug.

"Ow! That's my head!" a familiar voice complained from inside the rug.

I hopped up immediately.

Cleopatra stepped back toward her balcony. "What kind of trickery is this?"

I smiled as pleasantly as I could. *Yep, we're going to end up in the dungeons.* "It's no trickery. It's my brother. Although sometimes they're one and the same." I tapped the rug. "George how did you get in there?"

"We're both in here," Ernest's muffled voice answered from the other end of the rug. "Help get us out."

I unrolled the rug, and my brothers popped out as the last bit covered the floor. Before I was able to ask any questions, George started to blurt out the story.

"We couldn't understand a word anyone was saying after you left, so we decided to go find you. They wouldn't let us back in the palace, but we saw these guys bringing rugs and furniture into the palace."

Ernest picked up the tale. "We heard one of them point to this rug and say the name 'Cleopatra.' So, when the workers weren't looking, we unrolled it and then rerolled it on ourselves."

I looked at Cleopatra, expecting her to call the guards at any moment. Instead of being angry, the queen stared at my brothers and the rug with a thoughtful expression on her face.

"Interesting approach," Cleopatra mused. "I'll have to remember that trick someday."

Cleopatra smiled at me. "You and your brothers are truly ingenious. But back to work. What can you tell me about my future?"

I knew that the time for stalling was over. I closed my eyes and began to chant:

"Oooooommmm. Oooooommmm."

"What kind of foolishness is this?" Cleopatra asked.

I was about to open my eyes, but George chimed in.

"Oh, you must let her concentrate, Your Highness. My sister is a very powerful seer, but she needs to focus. She has traveled far and wide and has prophesized for kings and queens, emperors and empresses, sultans and...um...all sorts of other rulers and such. I am surprised that you have not herd of the Great Consantini."

Thank you, George. If anyone can make up a bunch of malarkey on the spot, it's my brother.

Now it was time for me to lay it on thick. I hummed and swayed. Then, in a monotone chant, I intoned, "I see you wearing the *pschent* and ruling over all of Egypt—"

"That's not a prophecy. I do that already," Cleopatra interrupted.

I cleared my throat. I wanted to tell the queen just where she could put her *pschent*, but then I thought about her vial of poison and that Cleopatra could do very mean things if she got upset.

Resuming my chant, I continued, "Yes, my queen, but in my vision you are not ruling with your father or brother, but by yourself," I continued.

"Oooo. Now that's more like it," Cleopatra said clapping her hands. "Tell me more."

"I see a boyfriend in your future. He is strong and powerful."

"Juba, King of Numidia?" Cleopatra asked.

"No, much stronger," I replied.

"King Orodes from the Parthian Empire?" the queen asked with excitement in her voice.

Geez, I feel like I'm hanging out with the typical, love-crazed teenager. "No, this man is from a much more powerful empire," I said, hoping I was taking this in the right direction. "Does the name Julius Caesar mean anything to you?"

Cleopatra responded with only silence, so I opened her eyes.

The pharaoh wore a nasty scowl and lowered eyebrows. No more lovesick teenager—back to nasty despot.

"I'm guessing you've heard of him?" Ernest asked.

"Yes," Cleopatra said slowly and icily. "He is a Roman general. A simple man. One not born with the divine right of kings."

"But he'll be very famous someday," George said. He was trying his best to sound encouraging. "And he'll rule the Roman Empire."

"Rome is not an empire; it's a republic," Cleopatra spat with venom in her voice. "Ruled by a sorry collection of commoners trying to be kings."

I scrambled through my brain for an answer. *Oh, no! That's right. During the time of Cleopatra, Rome was a republic, not an empire. That means that Rome was ruled by people elected into office, rather than having an emperor or king. The first emperor was actually Julius Caesar's nephew, Augustus. He was crowned in 27 BC. That's when the Roman Republic became the Roman Empire. And that's about twenty-five years from now...*

Cleopatra was shaking with anger.

The shaking wasn't so bad. What came next made me look for the closest exit.

"Guards! Guards!" Cleopatra yelled. "Take these slaves away and lock them in the dungeons forever and ever, until they are nothing but dust and bone!"

"Um, that doesn't sound pleasant. Let's get out of here!" George urged as he dashed toward the balcony.

"Let's hope that we're not too high up to jump for it," Ernest said, close at George's heels.

We held hands and leaped over the balcony wall. My stomach lurched, and I prayed that I wouldn't break my legs.

Chapter 11

A Light at the End of the Road

Luckily, Cleopatra's room was only on the second floor. We hit the ground and took off through the palace grounds and out into the city.

Alexandria was a great place to hide. People, animals, and carts crowded the narrow streets.

~ Constance Gatsby

The problem was that we had absolutely no clue how to get back to the canal. Let me take it from here.

~ Ernest Gatsby

George ducked under a hawker's display of low-hanging carpets. "Which way do we go?"

"These alleyways all look the same," Constance complained. "I feel like a mouse in a maze."

"Maybe we'll find a piece of cheese at the end," George said.

How my brother could think of a corny comment while we were running for our lives absolutely boggled my mind.

I gritted my teeth. "This is turning out just as I expected. We're going to die."

"We're not going to die," Constance said. "Look! There's water up ahead. It could be the canal."

I was dubious. "I don't know..."

The alley ended at a long, narrow causeway that led to an island. On the island, the gigantic Lighthouse of Alexandria towered above the sea.

"This isn't the right way," I said. "Let's go back."

Shouts rang out behind us.

"They went that way!"

"I think I see them!"

Cleopatra's soldiers pushed their way through the crowd, indiscriminately knocking over animals, carts, and people alike.

Not having any other choice, my siblings and I ran down the causeway. I dared a glance over my shoulder when we were halfway across. The palace guards exited the alley and were heading straight for us!

The lighthouse was surrounded by a tall wall, but thankfully the gates were open. We ran through the gates and into the lighthouse.

"Wait!" I said, stopping at a set of stairs that led up to the second floor. "Unless you plan on sprouting wings, we can't keep going this way. They'll catch us when we reach the top."

Constance shrugged. "Where else can we go? Maybe there'll be a place to hide on one of the floors. If they pass us, we can sneak back down while they keep climbing higher and higher."

I grimaced. "Or they could chase us to the top and then shove us over the edge. I don't want to end up as fish food."

"There they are!" a soldier shouted as he ran through the entrance gate. "Get those kids!"

That was all the incentive we needed. We ran up the stairs to the second level, hoping to find a place to hide, but it was an empty room with windows all around and another stairway leading farther up the lighthouse.

"They definitely need a decorator," George said.

Up and up we climbed. Each floor was the same as the last. My legs were on fire. I wasn't sure how many more stories I could climb, but the sound of the soldiers' pursuing feet kept me going.

Finally, we reached the top. We startled the lighthouse keeper, who jumped back as we reached the top platform

"Who are you?" he asked. "And what are you doing all the way up here?"

George stepped in front of Constance and I. "My companions and I are members of LIT—the Lighthouse Inspection Team. We're here to make sure that you know what you're doing."

"I have been the keeper of this lighthouse for twenty years. Of course I know what I'm doing," the man replied.

The sound of marching feet was getting closer.

"Prove it," George said with folded arms. "Cleopatra is on her way and expects to be satisfied with my report."

The man gulped. "Cleopatra...um...of course. Well, first, this is the brazier where we light the fires for the night."

"How about during the day?" George asked sharply. "I saw some bright flashes of light. What made that?"

The man pointed to a large mirror. "I turn it every few minutes so that ships out at sea can be guided to the harbor. Even during the brightest day, this light can be seen for many miles. But be careful near it. It's reflecting the light of the sun from that other mirror above us. If you look straight into this mirror, you'll be seeing spots for a week."

I looked up. There was a hole in the roof. A bright shaft of sunlight shone down and reflected off the mirror. My inventor's brain drooled at the prospect of being so close to such an amazing machine. I wanted to examine the mirror, see how it rotated, and know how they designed it. But there was a troop of soldiers after us...

"That's just what I needed to know," George said with a smile.

The footsteps were almost at the top of the stairs.

George ran behind the mirror and swiveled it on its base. "Duck!" he shouted as he aimed the mirror at the top of the stairs.

Constance and I jumped out of the way not a second too soon. A blinding beam of light engulfed the top of the stairs just as Cleopatra's soldiers reached the top step.

"What's going on?" one of the soldiers cried.

"I can't see!" yelled another.

This was great, but now what? The soldiers were still on the steps. And that was our only way down.

"Do you think we can sneak by them?" I asked George.

My little brother shrugged. "It's worth a try. Anyway, it's the only chance we've got."

Cleopatra's soldiers stumbled around the topmost room of the lighthouse, blindly groping for any hold of my siblings and I that they could get.

We were just about to make it past them when the lighthouse keeper finally caught on to our ruse.

"Wait a minute!" He exclaimed. "There's no Lighthouse Inspection Team. You're imposters!"

He swiveled the mirror and jumped in front of the stairs, blocking our exit.

What happened next is still a blur in my memory. All I can remember is that we ran around like crazy trying to get by wildly flailing soldiers with sharp spears and a very upset lighthouse keeper. There was a circular balcony that ran around the outside of the lighthouse. We must have run around it at least a half dozen times when somebody finally grabbed Constance by the collar and lifted her off her feet.

"You're not going anywhere, slave," the Egyptian soldier said. He swung my sister out over the balcony. "Queen Cleopatra doesn't take kindly to those who displease her."

Chapter 12

An Unexpected Pardon

I don't scare easily, but being held by a muscle-bound soldier on the top of a massive tower with my legs swinging hundreds of feet above the ground ...

Yeah, I almost wet my pants.

~ Constance Gatsby

Ernest and George stopped running. The other soldiers and the lighthouse keeper closed in on them.

"Run! Don't let them take all of us!" I yelled.

"Um, we kinda can't go anywhere without you," Ernest said.

"Yeah. You've got the you-know-what." George pointed to my pocket.

Ugh, that's right, I thought. *I've got the pendant.*

"All for one, and one for all," George said as he raised his hands above his head in surrender.

"I'm glad you're quoting something other than *Star Wars*," Ernest mumbled, raising his hands as well.

In a matter of seconds, the soldiers had captured my brothers, holding them fast with their hands behind their backs. They marched us down the many flights of the Lighthouse of Alexandria.

I tried to come up with a way to escape, but my mind felt numb. All I could think of was how stupid we were for doing this. Ernest was right. This was a mistake. A big mistake.

We continued across the causeway back into the city of Alexandria. With each step my stomach felt like it was getting tied into a tighter and tighter knot. *What was Cleopatra going to do with us?* Nothing I could think of was good.

We were doomed. Utterly doomed.

We rounded a corner and came within sight of the small canal where our Egyptian adventures all began. The washer woman was there again with her cart and a fresh load of dirty laundry.

An idea suddenly sprouted in my mind. It was a long shot. Totally desperate. But it was all I could think of.

I tapped the soldier next to me gingerly on the shoulder.

He spun around and lifted his spear. His thin beard framed a nasty scowl.

I couldn't help but take a step backwards. "Um. That washer woman has our clothes from our native land. We had left them with her. Could we get our clothes before we go back to the palace?"

The bearded soldier whispered to the soldier next to him. They exchanged a couple of words, then the second man nodded.

The first soldier, Mr. Nasty Beard, motioned to the washer woman. "Be quick, but go alone. I don't want you running away again. If you escape, your brothers will be at Cleopatra's mercy." He glowered. "And mercy is not something our queen is known for."

I gulped and ran to the washer woman.

As if anticipating my request, the woman grabbed our duffle bags from her cart and handed them to me as soon as I reached her.

"Good luck to you," she whispered. The washer woman bent her head back down to her work and said no more.

When I returned to my brothers, Mr. Nasty Beard ripped the duffle bags from my hands.

"Hey! Give them back!" I demanded.

The soldier ignored me and attempted to open my bag. Apparently, zippers were beyond the learning of ancient Egyptians. He pulled and prodded and shook my duffle bag until he was red in the face.

"Oh, give me that before you hurt yourself," I said as I pulled the duffle bag from his hands.

I unzipped the bag and handed it back to him.

Nasty Beard peered inside, and his brow wrinkled in confusion. He reached in and pulled out my tweed jacket. He held it up to show the others. Then my desperate plan actually started to work.

The Egyptian soldiers all began to laugh.

"What ridiculous clothing!"

"Who would wear that?"

"Make them try it on!"

That was what I was hoping to hear. My brothers and I scrambled through the pile of clothes that the soldier had dumped on the stone street. We kept them entertained and laughing by doing silly dances and pretending to get stuck and have trouble putting on our shirts and pants over our Egyptian clothing. In actuality, we got dressed faster than ever before.

Now all we needed was a chance to slip into the canal without getting skewered by an Egyptian spear.

Just as we finished replacing our sandals with our shoes, the sound of horses' hooves rang on the stones. Cleopatra's voice called out, "Where are they? Did you capture them?"

The young pharaoh approached riding a golden chariot pulled by a pair of magnificent white horses. She reined the horses to a stop, and a team of servants ran to either side of her, holding palm fronds to protect their queen from the sun.

The soldiers quickly regained their composure and seized my brothers and I anew. Mr. Nasty Beard held me tighter than ever, but this time his hands were quivering with fear for his ruthless queen.

"Slaves will not make a fool of me," the young pharaoh seethed. "They will pay for this. They will…"

Cleopatra's voice trailed off. She stepped off the chariot and patted her horse. "Stay," she commanded.

Ernest was right, I thought. *We're all going to die.*

Cleopatra stepped in front of us and stared at my brothers and I with a look of amazement. Gingerly, she touched our tweed jackets, one at a time. "You...you remind me of someone." Her hand strayed to the pendant around her neck— the one that our father would discover in an archeological dig 2,000 years in the future. Cleopatra continued as if talking to herself. "I haven't seen her since I was a little girl. She was very kind to me, and I..."

Turning to the soldiers, Cleopatra commanded, "Let them go."

"But, my queen, I don't understand," Nasty Beard said.

"You don't need to understand. You need to *obey*," Cleopatra snapped.

The soldiers immediately released us then retreated to positions around the pharaoh's chariot.

Cleopatra's expression softened as she addressed my brothers and me. "Go. I know that you can't stay. Go freely and safely." With those final words, Cleopatra returned to her chariot and rode off in the direction of the palace followed by her troop of trotting servants and soldiers.

"What was *that* all about?" Ernest asked.

George scratched his head. "Yeah, first she wants to lock us away forever. Next, we're free to go."

"Are you complaining?" Ernest asked.

"Nope. Absolutely not," George replied hastily.

"I guess it's time to go home now," I said.

My brothers nodded in agreement. We joined hands and walked into the river, leaving a very startled washer woman in our wake.

Chapter 13
An Explanation

Later that evening, back in good ol' Dayton, Ohio, we found our father in his study. Various objects from his latest Egyptian dig were strewn about the table in the center of the room— including Cleopatra's pendant, which I had successfully put back before he had arrived home from work.

"Hi, Dad! Whatcha up to?" George asked good-naturedly.

"Anything we can help with?" I asked.

"I don't think you can help me with this, unless you are an expert on hieroglyphs," Dad sighed. He held up the pendant. "See? Cleopatra probably wore it on a chain around her neck. It looks like a pair of columns with...I don't know...maybe a bird. This little triangle could represent a beak."

I cleared my throat. "What if Cleopatra didn't care about what others saw?"

Dad shook his head. "Oh, I'm not sure about that. Cleopatra was a very powerful ruler. What others saw would be very important."

"Could I hold it?" I asked.

Dad nodded. "Here. But please be careful with it."

I took the pendant and held it by the hoop. "Others would see it like this. But whenever Cleopatra looked at it, the pendant would look like this." I turned the pendant upside down.

"Now that's a nice thought, but I don't…" my father trailed off. His eyes opened wide, and he lifted the pendant closer to his face. "Well, I'll be…"

"What is it, Dad?" Ernest asked.

My father didn't take his eyes off the pendant as he spoke. "It's so simple. I can't believe that I didn't notice it before, but it still doesn't make any sense."

"Come on. Spill the beans," George insisted.

Dad traced the outside edge of the pendant. "This is the Greek letter *pi*—our letter P. This symbol hanging in the middle is the Egyptian letter G."

"PG? Maybe she liked going to the movies," George suggested.

"Yeah, sure," Ernest said rolling his eyes. "I can just see the marquis: Papyrus Pictures presents: *The Queen of the Nile*."

"Her father's name was Ptolemy. Maybe it's her father's and mother's initials," I suggested.

Dad scratched his head. "It's a thought. Ptolemy is the family name. But no one knows who her mother was."

"How about G for Gatsby?" George suggested.

"Oh, sure," Ernest scoffed. "Like *that* would make sense."

I smiled. "I'm sure you'll figure it out, Dad." I cleared my throat and grabbed my brothers by the sleeves. "Let's let him get back to his work."

We walked out of the study, leaving our father scratching his head and staring at Cleopatra's pendant.

"What did you do that for?" George asked.

"Yeah, we want to help him figure it out," Ernest protested.

I gave them a secretive look and ushered my younger brothers into my bedroom. "Grab a chair. You're going to need to be sitting down for this."

Ernest and George sat at the game table in the center of the room. They stared at me as I paced back and forth. Finally, I spoke.

"George, you were right."

George smiled. "Of course I was right." Then he paused. "Right about what?"

"I think the G on Cleopatra's pendant stands for Gatsby," I answered.

Ernest stood up. "Come on, George. Let's go help Dad. Constance is nuts."

I pushed my brother back down into his chair. "I'm not nuts. When I was in Cleopatra's private chamber—"

"We were *all* there," Ernest interrupted. "That's when you almost got us killed by telling her about Julius Caesar."

"Then why did she let us go?" I asked with a raised eyebrow.

George jumped into the conversation. "She liked our duds," he said pulling on the lapels of his jacket.

"And why did she like our clothing?" I pressed further.

"Um…" George hesitated.

"What does it matter?" Ernest asked. "We're back, we're alive, and we're never time-traveling again. Come on, George. Let's go help Dad."

Ernest stepped out of the room, dragging George behind him.

I remained silent as I sat on the edge of my bed. I thought back on the image of the little person standing next to Cleopatra on the wall of the pharaoh's private chambers. The little person wearing what looked like a checkered robe. Or could it have been a plaid tweed jacket? Just like the ones my brothers and I wore…

Dear Reader,

I hope you had fun reading this second book of the Gatsby Kids adventures. Constance, Ernest, and George have become like members of my family, and it is my sincere wish that you have delighted in bringing them into your life, too. Be sure to join them on their next adventure, *The Gatsby Kids Take a Ride on the Not-So-Underground Railroad*, in which they accidentally travel back to the 1800s and find a most intriguing clue about their past.

If you enjoyed *The Gatsby Kids Meet the Queen of the Nile*, please take the time to leave a review on Amazon or Goodreads. I would truly appreciate it.

For more book news or to contact me, please visit my website, www.bgmichaud.com or "like" my page on Facebook (Brian G. Michaud)—or both. ☺

Sincerely,
Brian G. Michaud

A Little More About Cleopatra

Cleopatra is one of the most famous women in history. She had a reputation for being ruthless, but she had to be in order to survive in the world in which she lived. In her defense, she was no worse than the male rulers that lived at the same time.

Cleopatra and her family, though pharaohs of Egypt, lived during a turbulent time in history when rulers were constantly going to war to either gain new territory or to keep what they had. The Ptolemies lived an erratic life—going from leadership to exile several times due to the growing power of ancient Rome. (Exile is basically being kicked out of your country.)

Cleopatra was born in 69 BC to her father Ptolemy XII and an unknown mother. In 58 BC a revolt sent her father into exile to several different countries, including Greece, until his return to the throne in 55 BC.[6] Cleopatra ruled from 52 BC to 51 BC with her father. (This is the point in Cleopatra's history when the Gatsbys meet her.)

Cleopatra's father died in 51 BC, and, according to his will, Cleopatra became co-ruler with her younger brother Ptolemy XIII. They had a falling out, and Cleopatra went into exile (again) in Syria where she amassed an army to overthrow her brother. Egypt fell into civil war from 49-47 BC because of this sibling rivalry. Cleopatra and

---

[6] Remember that when we refer to BC, "Before Christ," the dates go in reverse order. The birth of Jesus Christ is considered year 1.

her armies eventually won, and Cleopatra became the sole ruler of Egypt until her death in 30 BC.

Despite her misgivings, Cleopatra did eventually become Julius Caesar's girlfriend. The story goes that she rolled herself up in a rug to sneak into his private chambers. Hmmmm…sound familiar? They dated for a while and were the most talked about couple in the ancient world. That is until a bunch of guys killed Julius. Then Cleopatra started dating Marc Anthony and *they* became the most talked about couple in the ancient world.

Having a piece of jewelry from Cleopatra's private collection is a figment of this author's imagination because her tomb has never been found. When and if it is ever discovered, it will be one of the most exciting archeological finds ever!

To learn more about Cleopatra and ancient Egypt, check out books at your local library or visit some of the links below.

Ancient Egypt for Kids

http://egypt.mrdonn.org

Ducksters Education Site

http://www.ducksters.com

National Geographic Kids

https://www.natgeokids.com

History for Kids

http://www.historyforkids.net

How to Count with Roman Numerals

If you like history (and football), you should know a little bit about how to read Roman numerals. Roman numerals were used throughout the ancient world from about the 8th century B.C. to the 1400s—quite a long time!

Each number is represented by a letter or group of letters. It may seem confusing at first, but once you get the gist of it, it's not hard to do. Let's start with the basics:

$$I=1$$
$$II=2$$
$$III=3$$

So far so easy, right? Now let's check out the Roman numeral for five.

$$V=5$$

Hey, what about 4? I'll get to that. Let's keep going.

$$VI=6$$

$$VII=7$$

$$VIII=8$$

I bet you already guessed that I'm going to skip nine and go right on to ten.

$$X=10$$

So far, you might have noticed that the big number comes before the little number (V+I=VI is the same as 5+1=6). To make 4, the little number comes before the big number.

$$IV=4$$

What? A little confused? Think of it this way: the numbers are saying, "1 less than 5 is 4." Can you do the same with X and I to make 9.

Yep, you guessed it.

IX=9

So let's recap:

I=1

II=2

III=3

IV=4

V=5

VI=6

VII=7

VIII=8

IX=9

X=10

The Gatsbys first meet Ptolemy XIII. We read that as Ptolemy the 13th. His father is Ptolemy XII. We read that as Ptolemy the 12th.

The Cleopatra that we all know and love (and sometimes fear) was actually the seventh Cleopatra in the Ptolemy family, so she was Cleopatra VII.

Here are a few more number in case you're curious.

L=50

C=100

D=500

M=1000

Where else do you see Roman numerals? Three of the most common places are clocks, king/queen/pope titles, and football. To test your knowledge of Roman numerals, let's take a look

at the New England Patriots' Super Bowl
appearances. The Patriots were in (as of 2018):

Super Bowl XX

Super Bowl XXXI

Super Bowl XXXVI

Super Bowl XXXVIII

Super Bowl XXXIX

Super Bowl XLII

Super Bowl XLVI

Super Bowl XLIX

Super Bowl LI

Check the next page to see if you can figure
out the numbers.

Answers:

Super Bowl XX (20)

Super Bowl XXXI (31)

Super Bowl XXXVI (36)

Super Bowl XXXVIII (38)

Super Bowl XXXIX (39)

Super Bowl XLII (42)

Super Bowl XLVI (46)

Super Bowl XLIX (49)

Super Bowl LI (51)

Did you get them all right? Congratulations! Now you're a Roman numeral expert.

Made in the USA
Columbia, SC
15 October 2018